UNDEAD PETS

FLIGHT OF THE
PUMMELED PARAKEET

For Mum—SH

For Amy and Sam the Man—SC

GROSSET & DUNLAP
Penguin Young Readers Group
An Imprint of Penguin Random House LLC

Text © 2013 by Sam Hay. Illustrations © 2013 by Simon Cooper. All rights reserved.
First printed in Great Britain in 2013 by Stripes Publishing. First published in the United States of America
in 2015 by Grosset & Dunlap, an imprint of Penguin Random House LLC, 345 Hudson Street, New York,
New York 10014. GROSSET & DUNLAP is a trademark of Penguin Random House LLC. Printed in the USA.

Library of Congress Cataloging-in-Publication Data is available.

ISBN 978-0-448-47800-5   10 9 8 7 6 5 4 3 2 1

UNDEAD PETS

PETS

FLIGHT OF THE PUMMELED PARAKEET

by Sam Hay

illustrated by Simon Cooper

Grosset & Dunlap
An Imprint of Penguin Random House

The story so far . . .

Ten-year-old Joe Edmunds is desperate for a pet.

But his mom's allergies mean that he's got no chance.

Then his great-uncle Charlie gives him an ancient Egyptian amulet that he claims will grant Joe a single wish . . .

But instead of getting a pet, Joe becomes the Protector of Undead Pets.
He is bound by the amulet to solve the problems of zombie pets so
they can pass peacefully to the afterlife.

And so the
trouble begins . . .

CHAPTER ONE

Joe grabbed a handful of strawberries and dropped them into the jug.

PLOP!

"Maybe a little more banana," he said, stirring the mixture with a long wooden spoon.

His best friend, Matt, was standing next to him, smashing a bag of ice cubes with a rolling pin. He glanced at the jug. "There's no room."

"A few more blueberries, then . . ." Joe was just searching along the countertop for the bowl of berries when something hit his cheek.

"Hey!" He spun around to find the most annoying boy in the class, Spiker, smirking back at him. In his hand was the bowl of blueberries.

"Want some more?" Spiker fired another berry in Joe's direction.

Joe and Matt both ducked.

"Ow!" Leonie, who was behind Joe, let out a shriek as the blueberry bounced off her head.

Another volley followed. Joe and Matt dodged out of the way.

"*Argh!*" groaned Leonie. She turned around to see who was throwing the fruit just in time for a big squishy berry to explode on her cheek.

"Ms. Bruce! Someone's throwing fruit at me!"

In the blink of an eye, Spiker slid the bowl of blue-berries away from him along the countertop like a cowboy barman serving drinks in a saloon. "It was Joe!" he shouted.

"What? No, it wasn't!" Joe cried.

"Joe Edmunds!" shouted Ms. Bruce from the other side of the classroom. "I'm surprised at you!"

"But I didn't do anything . . ."

"It was Spiker!" Matt added.

Ms. Bruce held up her hand to silence them both. "Finish what you're doing, then bring your mixture over to the blender. It's your turn next."

It was Friday morning and the sixth grade students were making fruit smoothies in their home economics class. There was going to be an official tasting at the end of the day by their principal, Mr. Hill. The best smoothie would win a prize!

"Hold it still," said Matt as he poured the bag of crushed ice into their mixture.

"What's your smoothie called?" asked Molly, peering over Joe's shoulder.

"Berry Blaster!" He scowled over at Spiker.

"Joe, Matt, hurry up!" called Ms. Bruce, who was supervising the blender. "Bring your jug over here."

Matt shoved in the rest of the crushed ice, and Joe picked up the jug.

Just then, something splattered on his head. He spun around, expecting to find Spiker lobbing more fruit at him. But Spiker was over by the trash can, getting some paper towels. Joe glanced around suspiciously. Who was it, then?

SPLAT!

"Hey!" Something else had landed on his head. Joe reached up and touched it. It was soft and squishy. He inspected his fingers. "Ugh . . ." It was white with black bits in it. It looked just like bird poo.

UNDEAD PETS

There was a loud squawk and a brightly colored bird flashed in front of him.

Joe gasped. He twisted around to see where it had gone. "Did you see that? It looked like a parakeet!"

"Very funny!" said Matt, taking the jug out of Joe's hand. "And there's a UFO landing in the playground! Come on, or Leonie and Natalie will grab the blender before us!"

"Wait! Look over there!" said Joe. "On top of the whiteboard."

But Matt wasn't listening. He was already helping Ms. Bruce tip their mixture into the blender. "Get the spoon," he called over to Joe. "There are some bits stuck at the bottom."

But Joe didn't move. He couldn't take his eyes off the bird. It was hopping along the top ledge of the whiteboard now, cocking its head and nervously looking around the room.

Joe blinked a few times. Why hadn't anyone

else noticed it? You couldn't miss it—a bright green parakeet with a big scar and one bulging red eye!

Must have gotten in through the window, Joe muttered to himself. Ms. Bruce always had the windows open. She said fresh air was good for you. But Joe figured she just couldn't stand the smell of Spiker's sweaty feet!

"Look!" said Joe as Ava walked past with a bag of apples. "It's a parakeet."

"What?" She glanced to where Joe was pointing, then rolled her eyes. "Very funny!"

"Hurry up, Joe!" Matt called from the blender.

"Hurry up, Joe!" echoed the bird in a high-pitched singsong voice.

Joe grinned. It was mimicking Matt!

Then suddenly it fluttered over, landing on Joe's head.

"Hey!" Joe said, trying to swat it away.

"Hey!" it repeated. "Kissy, kissy!"

"Stop that!" Joe tried to wriggle free.

"Stop that!" copied the parakeet. "Who's a pretty boy?" it twittered. Then it dug its feet into Joe's scalp.

"Get off!" Joe yelled.

Ava glanced up from the workbench and nudged her twin sister, Molly. They were looking at Joe like he was nuts! Others were staring, too . . . Leonie giggled. Bethany pointed.

Joe was just about to shout to Ms. Bruce when the bird fluttered down from his head and hovered in front of his nose. It blinked a few times, then cocked its head at him.

"Sorry about that, Joe—just had one of my funny turns!"

"What?"

"My name's Petey, and I need your help!"

CHAPTER TWO

Joe gazed into the parakeet's single staring eye. "You're a zombie!" he whispered. That was all he needed! Another crazy undead pet—stuck in limbo land between this life and the next until someone solved its problems. And thanks to a magical Egyptian amulet that his great-uncle Charlie had given him, that someone was Joe!

He sighed. It wasn't even as if he could ask the parakeet what he wanted—not with everyone watching!

UNDEAD PETS

Just then, Matt turned on the blender . . .

SQUAWK!

The noise made Petey shoot up in the air like a firework. He hit the ceiling, then flapped jerkily across the room before bumping into a pile of apples and crash-landing in the twins' smoothie mixture!

PLOP!

Thick green goo splattered all over the worktop—and the girls!

"What was that?" yelled Molly.

"Yuck!" groaned Ava. Their shirts were covered in lumps of kiwi.

Petey bobbed up to the surface of their smoothie mixture, coughing and spluttering. He hauled himself over the edge of the jug . . .

SPLAT!

He landed on the worktop—a soggy ball of green goo.

Joe gulped. No one except him could see the undead pets—but people couldn't miss the mess they made.

"Was that you?" snapped Ava, glaring at Joe. "Did you chuck something in to our jug?"

"What?" Joe could barely hear her over the noise of the blender.

"Was it a tangerine?" Molly yelled. She peered into the mixture to see what had landed in there.

"I didn't chuck anything!" shouted Joe just as the blender stopped. The room was suddenly silent. Everyone turned and stared at him.

Ms. Bruce frowned. "What's going on?"

"Joe threw something into our smoothie!" wailed Ava. "Look at the mess!"

Spiker snickered.

"I didn't!" said Joe. "Honestly, I'll show you." He picked up a wooden spoon. He was about to use it to stir Molly and Ava's smoothie mixture, to prove there was nothing in there that shouldn't be, when his foot slipped on the smoothie splatter and he lost his balance. As he grabbed hold of the worktop to steady himself, he knocked into the twins' jug and it toppled off the bench . . .

A gigantic puddle of lumpy green goo spread across the floor. For a second, no one spoke. And then . . .

"Our smoothie!" wailed Molly.

"Way to go, Joe!" yelled Spiker, who was jumping up and down with excitement.

Then suddenly the whole class was roaring with laughter.

SQUAWK!

Petey took flight and flapped soggily back

up to the top ledge of the whiteboard, where he shook out his feathers and began twittering, "Time for tea! Good boy, Petey! See a penny, pick it up. All day long you'll have good luck!"

Joe looked at Petey, then at the sea of smoothie spreading across the floor. He wished the ground would swallow him up!

UNDEAD PETS

"Couldn't you have waited until after school?" grumbled Joe as he headed to the cafeteria to borrow a mop and bucket.

"There's no time!" said Petey, who had stopped twittering gibberish and was perched on Joe's shoulder, rocking back and forth like he needed to go to the bathroom. "You've got to help me—now!"

"Why?" said Joe. "What's the rush?"

"My owner, Maggie, is about to lose five hundred dollars!"

"What?"

"Her sister's going to steal it!"

Joe stopped. "Really? Her sister?"

Petey nodded. "Unless we stop her, Maggie will lose the money!"

"That's awful!" Joe thought for a moment. "Wait a minute! How do you know?"

"How do you know?" repeated Petey.

"How do you know?" Joe frowned. Petey's mimicking was beginning to get a bit annoying!

Petey cocked his head to one side. "Because I heard Maggie's sister say so! They live together."

"But why was the sister talking about it? That's not very smart."

They'd reached the door to the cafeteria. Joe could hear the lunch ladies clanking pots inside. "You'll have to tell me about it later—I've got to borrow a mop and bucket now, or I'll be in even more trouble with Ms. Bruce—"

"Wait!" shrieked Petey. "You don't understand."

"Later!" said Joe firmly, and he knocked loudly on the door.

"But Maggie is in that kitchen!" cried Petey. "And so is her sister!"

The kitchen door swung open and one of

the lunch ladies appeared—red-faced and smelling like onions.

"Yes? What do you want?" she asked.

"That's her!" tweeted Petey. "That's Maggie, my owner!" Then he started whistling loudly and chirping, "Kissy, kissy! Petey loves Maggie, kissy, kissy!"

Joe gulped. It was Ms. Pringle. Ms. Maggie Pringle. The Pringle sisters, Maggie and Pauline, were lunch ladies at Joe's school. Although they were sisters, they were very different.

UNDEAD PETS

Maggie was loud and round, with bright pink cheeks and wild curly gray hair that was always escaping from her hairnet. Pauline was smaller and spiky-looking. She never went anywhere without a thick smudge of bright red lipstick and a big squirt of stinky perfume.

"Yes? What is it?" Maggie boomed again.

Joe gulped. "Um, Ms. Bruce would like to borrow a mop and bucket, please."

"Pauline!" shouted Maggie. "Get a mop and bucket. Beverley needs it in grade six!"

Joe frowned. It was weird to hear Ms. Bruce referred to as "Beverley"!

"Wait there!" said Maggie. She bustled back into the kitchen, half closing the door behind her.

"Do something, Joe!" chirped Petey. "Go in there and tell Maggie what Pauline's planning!"

"Are you crazy? I can't do that!"

Inside, he could hear Pauline huffing and

UNDEAD PETS

puffing, moaning about being too busy to go get mops and buckets.

"They're always squabbling," Petey said with a sigh.

Just then, the door opened and a mop was thrust under Joe's nose, closely followed by a heavy metal bucket.

"Bring them back when you're finished," said Pauline. And she slammed the door shut.

"I still don't understand how Pauline could steal from her own sister," whispered Joe.

"They don't like each other!" explained Petey. "They're so different."

"How?"

"Maggie is a real saver. She loves a good bargain . . ." Petey seemed to drift off, daydreaming about Maggie. "Two-for-one! Good deal, Petey! Maggie likes a bargain! Good—"

"Hey!" interrupted Joe.

"Take care of the pennies, and the dollars will take care of themselves!"

"Petey!"

"What? Oh yeah . . . What was I saying?"

"About Maggie?"

"She's wonderful! She liked to stay home and play with me. She taught me to speak, and to sing songs and nursery rhymes. She loved my singing! Sometimes she'd give me a treat when I sang to her. *Round and round the garden, like a teddy bear. One step, two step, tickly under there!*"

"Petey! Concentrate!" Joe said.

"Sorry!" Petey squawked. "I miss Maggie, that's all!"

"What about Pauline?" said Joe.

"What about Pauline?" mimicked Petey. "What about Pauline!" Then he made a grumpy face. "She's always out! Shop, shop, shop! Silly Pauline! Shops till she drops! She's never got any money—she spends it all. That's why she's going to steal Maggie's prize! I tried to stop her, but I couldn't, and now look at me!"

Joe glanced up the corridor to check whether anyone else was coming. He had to make sure no one heard him speaking to Petey! "What do you mean?" he asked. "Did Pauline *kill* you? And what's this about a prize?"

"Well, it was last Saturday morning," began Petey. "Maggie was upstairs taking a bath when a letter arrived for her. Pauline was on her way to go shopping. She opened it by mistake— they've got the same last name, so it happens a lot."

Joe picked up the mop and bucket. "Go on, tell me the rest while we walk back to class."

The letter said Maggie had won
$500 in a department-store raffle . . .

I'll collect the raffle money
and keep it for myself!

Pauline put the letter in her
pocket.

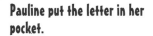

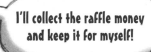

I'll collect the raffle money
and keep it for myself!

I like copying people. So I said
it, too.

Pauline was scared Maggie would hear me. She made a grab for me...

SPLAT!

I tried to escape, but I didn't see the window. I smashed straight into it!

Joe grimaced. "Is that why your flying is a bit wonky?"

Petey nodded. Then he began to twitter again. *"Sing a song of sixpence, a pocket full of rye. Four-and-twenty blackbirds, baked in a pie!"*

"I think the bump's made your brain wonky, too," mumbled Joe. Then, in a louder voice, he said, "So what happens now? What about the prize money? Doesn't Pauline have to go and collect it or something?"

Petey stopped twittering. "I dunno."

They'd arrived outside the classroom, and Joe could see the rest of the class cleaning up.

"Maybe Pauline's already got the money," said Joe. "Maybe you're too late."

Petey cocked his head to one side. "No! I've been following her."

"What? Spying on her?"

Petey nodded. "There's still time to stop

her! That's why I need your help—to get the letter back and give it to Maggie!"

"What?" Joe gulped. "Steal it, you mean?"

"Yes, from Pauline's coat pocket!" Petey nodded solemnly. "Her coat's in the school kitchen, Joe. You have to go and get it. It's the only way!"

CHAPTER THREE

While the rest of the class drew labels for their smoothie mixtures, Joe got started cleaning up the big green puddle. He heaved another mop full of soapy water onto the classroom floor and sighed. He couldn't think how to help Petey. And he really did want to help him—and Maggie. After all, he knew what it was like to have an annoying sister. But there was no way he was going to steal a letter from someone's coat!

"You missed a spot," sneered Spiker,

deliberately walking through the green goo so he could spread it across the floor.

"Get lost!" Joe flicked the soapy mop at him.

Matt appeared holding a wad of paper towels. "Hey, our smoothie tastes amazing, by the way," he said.

"Great!" Joe dunked the mop back into the bucket. "Maybe we'll win!" Then he spotted the twins in the corner, sticking labels on empty plastic bottles. "What about Ava and Molly?"

"They made another batch," said Matt. "With everyone's leftovers."

Joe watched the girls pour a jug of orangey brown liquid into one of the bottles. He felt bad that Petey had ruined their smoothie. He glanced around the room. Where *was* Petey, anyway?

Then he heard a strange tapping sound and spotted the small parakeet sitting next to

the mirror above the sink, pecking it.

"Kissy, kissy," he chirped. "Kissy, kissy, for Petey boy!"

Joe rolled his eyes. What a birdbrain!

"Well done, Joe!" said Ms. Bruce, who'd come over to inspect the floor. "You've done a good job. You'd better take the mop and bucket back now." She looked at her watch. "Be quick! The lunch ladies will be getting ready to serve lunch soon!" Ms. Bruce turned to the rest of the class. "Everyone else, go and wash your hands."

Joe headed for the door, the dirty water in the bucket slopping over the sides.

"Wait for me!" squawked Petey, swooping down to land on Joe's shoulder and gripping with his claws. Joe winced. Joe was beginning to feel like a pirate with a bothersome parrot stuck to his shoulder!

He headed down the corridor toward the kitchens just as the lunch bell rang and classroom doors sprang open.

"Watch it!" muttered a girl as Joe bumped into her with the bucket, splashing dirty green water on her tights.

"Sorry," he said, doing his best to dodge through the crowds.

As they reached the kitchen door, Petey pecked his ear. "Are you going to get the letter now? Pauline's coat's in there!"

"No! I told you, I can't just steal it." He knocked loudly.

After a few minutes, the door was flung open and Maggie stood there, her face even redder than last time. She glanced at the mop. "Just shove it in the closet over there," she said, pointing to the back of the kitchen. Then she grabbed a tray of fries off the counter and bustled away, through the door to the cafeteria.

"Quick, Joe!" squawked Petey. "Now's your chance!"

Joe hesitated. He'd never been in the kitchen before. It was strictly out of bounds to students. He glanced at the enormous steaming pots bubbling on the stovetop and the huge metal jugs of gravy lined up, ready to be taken to the cafeteria.

"Don't just stand there!" said Maggie, who'd reappeared. "You'll miss your lunch! Stick the mop in the closet!" Then she grabbed two jugs full of gravy and rushed off again.

"Come on, Joe! Pauline's coat's in the same closet!" Petey took off, flying unevenly across the kitchen. "Over here!"

Joe followed nervously, dragging the mop and bucket with him.

UNDEAD PETS

Petey was hovering in front of the closet. "Quick, Joe! Get the letter!"

With a slightly sweaty hand, Joe pulled open the door. Inside were some brooms and, hanging up, two coats . . .

Joe gulped.

"That's Pauline's!" squawked Petey, fluttering around a puffy purple jacket. "Look! There's something in the pocket!"

Joe swallowed hard. This felt all wrong.

"Go on, Joe! What are you waiting for?"

But Joe couldn't do it. Even though the letter rightfully belonged to Maggie, not Pauline, he still felt like a thief!

"Hurry!" trilled Petey. "You've got to help Maggie!"

Joe reached out and took the piece of paper. It was a letter from Beddows—the big department store in the center of town.

B

Beddows

CONGRATULATIONS!

You are the winner of the grand prize in the Beddows raffle!
Please bring your raffle ticket to our store to collect your prize!
$500

UNDEAD PETS

Before Joe could read any more, he heard footsteps behind him. He jammed the letter back in Pauline's coat pocket and spun around. But he'd forgotten about the mop . . .

He tripped and stumbled, then lost his balance, landing bottom down in the bucket! Cold, soapy green water seeped through his pants.

"What's going on?"

Joe looked up into the shocked face of Pauline Pringle.

"What are you doing in here?" she demanded.

"Ms. Bruce said I should bring back the mop and bucket. I knocked at the door and Ms. Pringle—I mean, the other Ms. Pringle—said I should put it in the closet. But then I sort of tripped over the mop and . . ."

Pauline rolled her eyes and pursed her bright red lips. "And got yourself stuck in the bucket!"

UNDEAD PETS

Joe struggled to his feet and the cold water dripped out of his pants and onto the floor.

"Mop it up," snapped Pauline, "then stick some newspaper down on the floor so no one slips on it." She opened a metal cabinet and pulled out a couple of old newspapers and a box marked LOST PROPERTY. "And you'd better borrow some dry clothes out of there!" Then she grabbed the rest of the gravy jugs and left.

Joe groaned. That was the last straw. Now he'd have to spend the rest of the day wearing someone else's clothes. And even worse, the only thing he could find in the box that was his size was an old pair of gray sweatpants that smelled like pee . . .

"What about the letter?" squawked Petey. "You need to give it to Maggie!"

"I can't!" hissed Joe. "In case you haven't noticed, I've got to clean up this mess! And anyway, Pauline could pop her head back in here anytime!"

He dunked the mop back into the bucket, gave it a swirl, then slopped it down onto the floor.

A few minutes later, Pauline reappeared carrying a stack of empty metal trays that she banged down on the kitchen counter. "That's enough mopping! Put down some newspaper, then go and get your lunch."

Petey was fluttering around Joe's head, clearly annoyed. "Do something, Joe! We've got to get that letter! As soon as she's gone, try again!"

But Pauline wasn't going anywhere. "I'll put it away!" she said, taking the mop out of Joe's hands and shoving it roughly into the closet. Then she turned to her coat, glanced furtively over her shoulder, took out the letter, and stuffed it in her apron pocket.

"The letter!" shrieked Petey. "She's taking away the letter!"

"Get a move on," said Pauline as she passed Joe. "Or there'll be nothing left to eat!"

Petey collapsed on the floor and buried his head under his wing. "We'll never get the letter now!" And then he started twittering again. *"Polly put the kettle on! Polly put the kettle on!"*

"Petey!" said Joe, trying to get his attention.

But the parakeet ignored him. "Kissy, kissy! Time for tea! *Happy birthday to you! Happy birthday to you!"*

"PETEY!" said Joe. "Snap out of it!"

But Petey didn't stop singing, and he began plucking out his green feathers, too. "She loves me, she loves me not. She loves me, she loves me not . . ."

"Stop it! You'll go bald!" Joe gritted his teeth and turned back to the wet floor.

As he put down a sheet of newspaper, he

UNDEAD PETS

spotted something—a large advertisement on the back page. It was for Beddows department store, advertising a special one-day super sale on Sunday to celebrate the store's fiftieth anniversary. But that wasn't what caught Joe's eye. It was the line at the bottom of the ad that made him sit up straight.

"Petey!" Joe gasped. "It's Maggie's prize!"

Petey stopped gibbering and his head spun around to look at Joe, his beak full of feathers.

"Wmmmph?" he mumbled.

Joe frowned.

"Sorry," Petey said, spitting out the feathers. "What did you say?"

"Look!" said Joe, pointing at the page. "It says here that the winner of the raffle will be presented with their prize on Sunday!"

Petey cocked his head and looked blankly at Joe.

"Don't you see? That must be Maggie's prize! She's supposed to collect it on Sunday. That means we've still got two days to find a way to stop Pauline!"

CHAPTER FOUR

"What kept you so long?" asked Ben as Joe came into the cafeteria and flopped down in the seat next to Matt.

"Don't ask," Joe groaned. He glanced around. There were a lot of empty places at the table, as most of the kids had already finished eating. Petey was hopping around on the table pecking crumbs. Joe was glad to have a break from him!

Matt made a face. "What's that smell? Why are you wearing those?" He pointed at Joe's sweatpants.

"It's a long story," said Joe, stabbing a carrot with his fork and looking at his food miserably.

The carrot was mushy, and the shriveled slice of pizza didn't look too tasty, either. He put down his fork.

"You're not leaving that, I hope!" Maggie Pringle loomed over him, a wet dishcloth in her hand. "That's good food. You shouldn't waste it!"

"It's cold," said Matt.

"And soggy," added Ben.

Undead Pets

"Others would be happy to get a meal like that," said Maggie solemnly. "Now eat it up like a good boy!"

Joe picked up a knife and tried to saw through the pizza crust.

"You need an ax," Ben said with a giggle.

"More like a chainsaw!" Matt replied with a snicker.

Maggie gave them a stern look, then went off to wipe down a table nearby.

"So, what's with the clothes?" asked Matt.

"I had an accident with the bucket," mumbled Joe. He was still trying to chew the lump of concrete pizza.

"What sort of an accident?"

"I fell in the bucket."

Ben snickered.

"Loser!" Matt grinned.

Joe used his finger to flick a small piece of pizza crust off his plate toward Matt.

"Hey!" Matt laughed. "Anyway, did I tell you I'm getting some new boots on Sunday?"

"What?" Ben stopped eating his pudding and frowned. "You're always getting new stuff!"

"There's a big sale—" began Matt.

"At Beddows department store?" Joe put in. "I heard about that."

"I wish my mom would buy me new boots," said Ben glumly.

"Tell her about the sale. There's free cake,

too!" said Matt. "I heard Mom telling my dad that he could go and eat cake while she went shopping!"

Suddenly a hand appeared in front of Joe and swiped his plate away.

"Had enough?" It was Pauline. She was piling empty plates onto a cart. She was about to scrape his pizza into a bucket of scraps when Maggie thundered over.

"Stop! He's not finished!"

Pauline looked at the plate, then at Joe, then at the clock on the wall. "Yes, he has. He should be eating the pudding by now!"

Maggie glared at her sister. "But look at all that good food going to waste!"

Pauline pursed her lips. "He was late for lunch, so it's his own fault if he doesn't have time to finish it. He's got to eat his pudding now!" She looked at the clock again.

Joe coughed. "Um, I'd had enough anyway."

The lunch ladies glared at him, then at each other.

Petey fluttered over and landed on Joe's shoulder. "It's always like this!" He sighed. "Bicker, bicker, argue, argue. I wish they'd put a sock in it!" He shook his head and flew off.

"Give him his plate back!" growled Maggie.

"No!" snapped Pauline.

Moments later, there was a loud bang on the other side of the room.

A large plastic water jug had fallen off the serving counter.

Maggie gave a loud sigh, then turned to go and sort it out. As soon as she'd gone, Pauline made off with the cart—and Joe's plate!

"Lucky escape!" Matt grinned.

"Yeah, I thought she was going to chain you in the kitchen until you'd finished it all!" Ben giggled.

Joe wolfed down his pudding, just in case Pauline came back. Then they trooped out of the cafeteria.

As they left, Petey fluttered down and landed on his shoulder again. "Smart boy, Petey! Petey's a smart boy!" Then he leaned over and whispered in Joe's ear, "I knocked over the water jug to make them stop arguing!"

Joe smiled.

Petey cocked his head to one side. "It was close to the edge—so I gave it a shove. Good boy, Petey! Petey is a smart boy!"

Perhaps Petey wasn't as much of a birdbrain as Joe had thought . . .

CHAPTER FIVE

"I still think we should have won!" grumbled Matt as he, Joe, and Joe's little brother, Toby, walked home from school.

"Won what?" asked Toby, who was walking along the edge of the curb as though it were a tightrope.

"The smoothie competition!" said Matt. He and Joe had been talking about nothing else since they'd left school, but Toby hadn't been listening.

"Who won it?" asked Toby.

"The twins!" said Joe and Matt together.

"I think Mr. Hill just felt sorry for them," said Matt. "Because they lost their first batch."

Joe glanced at Petey out of the corner of his eye. The parakeet was hopping up and down on his shoulder, whistling tunelessly.

"Want to come over to my house and play Xbox tonight?" asked Matt.

"I can't," said Joe. "I'm helping Mom with the flyers for her new business."

"Huh?" Matt looked at him blankly.

"You know—my mom's new hairdressing business."

Matt shrugged.

"She's left the hair salon and set up on her own. She's going to cut people's hair in their own homes."

"Oh, right," said Matt. "And you're going to be doing that all night?"

"Yeah, well, I said I'd help her sort out the

flyers she's had printed. We're going to put them in people's mailboxes tomorrow to try and get her some customers."

"What?" Petey stopped whistling and gave a squawk. "But you've got to go over to Maggie's house tomorrow and find that letter!"

Joe ignored him. "She's paying me," he added. "Hey, do you want to help deliver them? I'll split the money with you."

Matt shrugged. "Okay."

UNDEAD PETS

Petey was shrieking now. "What about Maggie? You need to get that letter!"

When Joe didn't reply, Petey pecked his ear.

"Yow!" Joe tried to bat Petey away, but he'd already taken off—fluttering lopsidedly up into the branches of a nearby tree, where he sat twittering angrily.

Joe rubbed his ear.

"What happened?" Matt asked.

"Wow!" said Toby, his eyes like saucers. "Your ear's bright red!"

"Um, something must have stung me," Joe mumbled.

"What? Like a killer bee?" Toby was peering at his ear now. "I saw some on TV! They stung a man's nose and it swelled up—and then it exploded!"

"Great!" Joe rolled his eyes. "Come on, Toby. Mom will be waiting . . ."

"Why did you peck me?" Joe asked.

Petey was sitting on top of the curtain pole in Joe's bedroom, his head tucked under his wing, muttering to himself. "Bad Petey. Petey is a bad, bad boy!"

Joe groaned. "Don't go all bonkers on me again!"

Petey shook his feathers. "Sorry! Sorry about pecking you . . . But I hate it when people ignore me!" He puffed up his little chest and let out a deep sigh. "What's the plan to stop Pauline?"

Joe sank down onto his bed. "I dunno." He glanced aimlessly around the room. Then his eyes rested on the magical Egyptian amulet Uncle Charlie had given him. It was small and black and shaped like a jackal. It was this amulet that had started all of his undead-pet troubles in the first place!

UNDEAD PETS

Joe reached over to pick it up, and spotted something underneath.

"Raffle tickets!"

Petey flew over to Joe.

"Look," said Joe. "These are raffle tickets I got from my soccer team. I've got to keep them safe until the drawing."

Petey shrugged. He still looked like his brain had gone on vacation.

"When I bought these tickets," explained Joe, "the soccer team kept one half of the ticket—the stubby bit. And they gave me the other half, see?" Joe showed Petey the tear down the side of each ticket. "The piece that the team kept is going into a hat, and when they've sold all the tickets, they'll pick one ticket out of the hat as the winner. But the drawing isn't till next month, so I've got to keep the tickets safe until then. If they draw my ticket out of the hat, then I have to show them this half of the ticket to prove I bought it! Don't you see?"

The parakeet shook his head.

"The letter in Pauline's pocket said that Maggie had to bring her winning raffle ticket to the store to receive her prize. That means she's probably got her part of the ticket in the house somewhere!"

"I get it! I get it!" Petey bobbed his head excitedly. "If we can find the ticket before

Pauline, she won't be able to get the prize!"

Joe sagged a bit. "But what if Pauline already has Maggie's half of the ticket as well as the letter? And anyway, there's no way I can get inside the house to look!"

Petey let out a long sad whistle. "We'll never stop Pauline!" Then he plucked out one of his feathers. "*One, two, buckle my shoe, three, four, knock at the door!*"

"Don't start saying all that silly stuff again!" said Joe. "And stop pulling out your feathers! You've already got a bald patch on your wing, you know!"

"*Five, six, pick up sticks, seven, eight, lay them straight!*"

PLUCK!
PLUCK! PLUCK!

Joe sighed. It was probably best to leave the bird alone.

UNDEAD PETS

He kicked off his shoes and pulled a pair of jeans out of his drawer. He couldn't wait to get out of the stinky "lost and found" sweats!

"Joe! What's this?" Mom stood in the doorway holding the plastic bag stuffed with Joe's wet clothes. "I found it in your book bag!"

Joe's face reddened. "It's my pants. I had a bit of an accident."

Mom gasped.

"No!" he said quickly. "I didn't wet myself! I sort of fell into a bucket of soapy water . . ."

"Oh, right," said Mom. "And how do you explain the lumps of kiwi?"

UNDEAD PETS

"Well, um, it was soapy water mixed with fruit smoothie—a kiwi and lime smoothie."

Mom smiled. "Of course it was! Why didn't I think of that?" She rolled her eyes.

Nothing Joe did seemed to surprise his mom anymore. He'd been in so much trouble lately that this sort of thing counted as normal behavior. And there was no way he could tell her that it was all thanks to the undead pets!

"When you're ready," Mom said, "would you come downstairs and help me sort out the flyers? I've had another idea for a promotion, too!"

"Oh yeah? What is it?" Joe asked.

"I'm going to knock on a few doors when we're delivering the flyers tomorrow and offer half-price, on-the-spot haircuts."

"What, on their front steps?"

Mom nodded. "Well, not actually on the

steps! Inside would be fine. What do you think?"

"Um . . ."

"Everyone loves a bargain, Joe!" said Mom.

"Everyone loves a bargain, Joe!" repeated Petey. "B.O.G.O.F., Petey! B.O.G.O.F.—buy one, get one free! Take care of the pennies, and the dollars will take care of themselves! Everyone loves a bargain, Joe."

Joe stared at Petey. Of course! Maggie was a total penny-pincher! She'd love a half-price haircut. All they had to do was knock on her door and offer it to her . . . then Joe would be able to get into her house and look for the raffle ticket!

The only trouble was, he had no idea where she lived.

CHAPTER SIX

Joe scrolled down the page of addresses and phone numbers he'd found online.

A. PRINGLE

A.A.R. PRINGLE

A.M. PRINGLE

C. PRINGLE

Rev. D. PRINGLE

D.W.J. PRINGLE

Dr. G. PRINGLE

"Oh no!" he groaned. "There are seven M. Pringles listed! How am I supposed to knock on seven doors?" He glanced at the addresses. He'd never even heard of half the streets. "They're probably spread out all over town."

Petey fluttered around Joe's head, then landed clumsily on his shoulder. The bird cocked his head and looked curiously at the computer.

"Do you recognize any of the addresses?" Joe nodded to the screen. But Petey just shrugged. Then Joe remembered Petey probably couldn't read. "What about this," Joe said, reading the first. "Number 11 Dover Sole Street?"

Petey began whistling tunelessly to himself.

"47 Hartley Road?"

Still nothing.

"Hang on," said Joe. "Pauline Pringle must be listed here as well. So if I can find a P. Pringle with the same address as an M. Pringle, then that's the one!"

He glanced up and down the list. "There!" he said. "29 Argyll Avenue?"

Suddenly, Petey squawked, "Petey Pringle, 29 Argyll Avenue, telephone number 555-6283!"

"What?" Joe glanced up.

Petey had hopped onto the shelf above the computer. "Petey Pringle, 29 Argyll Avenue, telephone number 555-6283."

"Is that where you live?"

"Petey Pringle, 29 Argyll Avenue, telephone number 555-6283."

"Petey!" said Joe. "Snap out of it!" He clapped his hands.

Petey jerked back to normal again.

"Did you live on Argyll Avenue?" asked Joe.

Petey nodded. "Maggie taught me to say my address in case I got lost."

Joe rolled his eyes. "Why didn't you say so? Birdbrain!" He grinned. "Argyll Avenue's not that far from here."

Petey began bobbing his head up and down, flapping his wings, and chirping. "Can we go? Can we go now?"

Joe shut down the computer. "Tomorrow, Petey. We'll go tomorrow."

"Not fish sticks again!" wailed Sarah.

It was dinnertime. Joe was sitting at the

table with Toby and his big sister, Sarah.

"Sorry," said Mom, who was peering at a street map she'd printed off the computer. "I've been too busy to go food shopping this week. So we're eating up what's in the freezer."

"I don't mind," mumbled Toby, his cheeks stuffed with fries. "I love fish sticks and french fries!"

Sarah scowled at him.

Mom picked up a yellow highlighter and drew a large circle around their neighborhood; then she drew a line down the middle.

"Is that where we're delivering the flyers?" asked Joe.

Mom nodded.

Joe pointed his fork at the section with Argyll Avenue in it. "Maybe you and me could do that part, Mom. And Matt said he'd help, too."

"No way!" snapped Sarah. "I'm doing Argyll

Avenue—that's where Gabriella lives."

Joe groaned. That's why he knew that street. Gabriella was Sarah's best friend. He'd been in the car when they'd dropped Sarah off for sleepovers at Gabriella's house.

"I'm sure Joe won't mind if you do Argyll Avenue," said Mom. "Will you, Joe?"

"Um, well . . ." Joe tried to think of a good reason to say no.

Petey, who had been sitting on the lampshade above their heads, shrieked suddenly. He dive-bombed down toward the table, knocking a layer of dust off the lamp and landing with a thud in front of Joe's plate. "Argyll Avenue? Argyll Avenue! That's Maggie's street. Tell her you're doing that one, Joe!"

Joe took a deep breath. "Mom, I have to do that street because I promised someone that I'd deliver a flyer to their house."

"Who?" demanded Sarah. "Who do you

know on Argyll Avenue?"

Joe racked his brain. Apart from Maggie and Pauline Pringle, there was no one!

"Well," said Joe, playing for time. He was trying to think of someone in his class that Sarah wouldn't know . . .

"No one!" declared Sarah. "He's just saying he wants to do Gabriella's street to annoy me." She shot him an evil look.

"Ms. Pringle from our school!" burst out Joe.

"Who?" asked Mom.

All eyes were on him now. Even Toby had stopped chewing and was peering at him.

"One of the lunch ladies from school," he mumbled. "I sort of told Ms. Pringle about your new business"—he tried to ignore Sarah's scowl—"and I said I'd be putting a flyer through her door. She was really excited to book an appointment."

"So what?" snapped Sarah. "I'll do it. There's no reason why *you* have to do it!"

"B-b-but . . ." Joe stuttered. "But—"

"Come on!" Sarah whined. "Why does it have to be you?"

Petey made a strange hissing noise. He was staring at Sarah. "She's mean!" he said. Then he flew at her and pecked her nose.

"Ow!" Sarah squealed.

"What is it?" Mom looked at Joe. "Did you throw something at Sarah?"

"No!"

"Maybe it was the same as what bit you, Joe!" Toby said.

"What?" Mom looked worried. "When did you get bitten, Joe?"

"Just on the way home from school. It might have been a flea . . ."

"A flea?" Mom looked appalled.

Joe gulped. "Yeah. Maybe the clothes I

borrowed from school had fleas?"

Mom gasped.

"Or maybe not," said Joe quickly.

"Mom! My nose!" wailed Sarah.

"Let me look." Mom leaned over the table. "Oh, it does look a bit red." She gave Joe a searching look. "Are you sure you didn't throw something at your sister?"

"Yes!"

Petey was back on the lampshade again, swinging back and forth, knocking off more dust.

Achoo!

Achoo! sneezed Mom as a little cloud of dust cascaded down. *Achoo! Achoo! Achoo!*

"Mom!" snapped Sarah. "What about my nose!"

Mom rubbed her eyes. "It looks okay now, Sarah." *Achoo!* Mom sneezed again. *Achoo! Achoo!*

"Tell Joe that I'm doing Argyll Avenue," said a frustrated Sarah.

Mom sighed. "How about we all do it," she said. Then she sneezed again!

"You've got to stop pecking people!" said Joe as he got ready for bed.

Petey, who was sitting on a model airplane that hung from Joe's ceiling, shrugged. "That's what parakeets do!"

"Not all of them!"

"She deserved it."

Joe couldn't argue with that.

"Night, Petey," he said, climbing into bed. "And don't let the bedbugs bite." He grinned. As soon as dinner was over, Mom had taken away the "lost and found" sweatpants and put them straight in the washing machine—just in case they really did have fleas.

Joe closed his eyes.

"Twinkle, twinkle, little star . . ."

Joe groaned.

"How I wonder what you are . . ."

"Petey!"

"Up above the world so high . . ."

"Stop it! I can't sleep with you babbling on."

"Baa, baa, black sheep—"

"PETEY!" Joe flicked on the light.

"Sorry, Joe, but Maggie and I always sang songs together before she put the cover over my cage." He looked around anxiously. "I don't think I can sleep with so much space around me."

UNDEAD PETS

"But I don't have a birdcage," Joe said. At this rate he wouldn't get a wink of sleep. "Wait a minute." Joe climbed out of bed and walked over to the closet. He rifled through piles of puzzles and games. "There!" He pulled out a large junk model made of old shoe boxes, yogurt containers and scraps of paper.

"What is it?" asked Petey uncertainly.

"It's a model T. rex. I made it when I was six. I got a prize for it at school!"

Petey looked at the creature curiously.

"There you go," Joe said, putting it on top of his dresser. "It's a bit like a birdcage."

Petey flew into the dinosaur's mouth and peeped out. "I can still see the room!"

Joe sighed. Then he grabbed his T-shirt and draped it over the model. "Good night, Petey."

There was no reply.

CHAPTER SEVEN

"Are you really going to knock on their door?" Matt still couldn't believe they were at the Pringle sisters' house.

It was Saturday morning, and they'd been delivering flyers since eight o'clock. Argyll Avenue was their last street before they took a break.

Sarah, who was doing Gabriella's side of the street with Toby and Dad, stuck her tongue out at Joe. "I bet I get a customer before you!"

Joe made a face back at her. "Come on,"

he said to Matt. Mom, who was handing over a flyer to the lady who lived in the house next door to the Pringles, gave Joe a hopeful thumbs-up. Lots of people were interested in booking appointments, but no one had wanted an instant haircut yet!

Joe rang the bell, his heart racing. Somehow he had to convince Maggie to get a haircut. And—most important—let him inside!

Petey was sitting on Joe's shoulder twittering nervously. "Who's a pretty boy? Petey boy! Petey boy! Kissy, kissy!"

Just then, the door opened. It was Maggie Pringle.

"Yes? What is it?" She frowned at Joe and Matt.

"MAGGIE!" squawked Petey with delight, fluttering over to perch near Maggie, even though she had no idea he was there.

Joe smiled politely. Maggie was wearing a bright orange cardigan, purple pants, and strange, fluffy bottle-green slippers. Her wispy hair was blowing around in the breeze. She stared at Joe for a moment, trying to place him.

"Hello, Ms. Pringle. It's Joe Edmunds, from school . . ."

"Yes? What do you want?"

Joe suddenly felt a bit tongue-tied.

"Would you like a half-price haircut?" blurted out Matt. "Right now!"

"What?" Maggie looked at him as though he were crazy. "You want to cut my hair?"

Joe tried not to laugh. "No! Not us— my mom." He handed her a flyer. "She's a hairdresser, and she's offering a special deal today—a front-door discount."

"A discount, you say?" Maggie peered at the flyer.

"Yeah, it's a special deal. Half-price haircuts if you get it done now!"

Maggie looked a bit shocked. "What? Right now?"

Joe nodded. "That's my mom over there." He waved over to her and she came to join them.

"Good morning!" She smiled. "I'm Helen Edmunds. I run a hairdressing business—I used to be the senior stylist at Cut Above."

Maggie nodded. "Oh yes, my sister goes there. It's expensive, though, isn't it?"

Joe glanced at Maggie's wild hair. It looked like she cut it herself—with garden shears!

"We're just handing out a few flyers," said Joe's mom. "It's half price if you have your hair cut now. It's a special introductory offer."

"I see," said Maggie. "Well, it sounds like a good deal." Maggie inspected the price list printed on the flyer and then smiled at Joe's mom. "Count me in!"

Mom beamed. "Great! I'll get my things from the car." She headed off before Maggie could change her mind, leaving Joe and Matt on the doorstep.

"I suppose you two will want to come in for some juice while your mom's cutting my hair?"

"No!" squeaked Matt. "We've got more flyers—"

Joe cut him off. "Thanks, Ms. Pringle. That would be great!"

Matt frowned at Joe, but didn't say anything.

"What's going on?" Pauline Pringle had appeared in the hall.

"I'm getting my hair cut!" said Maggie. "I'll just grab a towel. I said I'd give the boys some juice. Would you mind, Pauline?"

Pauline pursed her lips and peered at Joe. "You again!"

"Hello, Ms. Pringle," said Joe nervously.

"His mom's going to give me a haircut," called Maggie as she headed upstairs.

Pauline looked puzzled. "Now?"

"You could get one, too," Matt suggested, handing her a flyer.

"Don't be ridiculous!" she muttered. "Go ahead." She nodded toward the living room.

Petey was already waiting for them. He had flown straight through the wall and was now flapping around the room in big loops. "Look for the raffle ticket, Joe! It must be here somewhere!"

But Joe wasn't sure where to start. The room was full of stuff! There were two flowery sofas, an old armchair, and lots of shelves and cabinets with ornaments inside.

Matt made a face. "Yuck!" he whispered. "Look at all this stuff—it's gross!"

"Maggie is very proud of her china," squawked Petey, agitatedly fluttering around Matt's head. "What does he know?"

An old-fashioned clock in the center of the mantelpiece chimed on the half hour. Joe jumped.

"Don't touch anything!" said Pauline, coming in carrying a tray with two small glasses of juice on it. "Sit down, and sit still!"

Joe's mom appeared with her bag of equipment. "Where shall I set up? Most people find that the kitchen's best."

Pauline nodded. "Follow me!"

"Find the raffle ticket!" squawked Petey.

"Do you think you should be touching that?" asked Matt as Joe started picking up the ornaments and looking at them.

Joe reached for a small ballerina figurine.

UNDEAD PETS

"Stop!" hissed Matt. "Ms. Pringle will go crazy if she sees you!"

Joe shrugged. "I was just wondering if they were . . . antiques."

"Since when did you become an expert?"

"Dad likes watching antique shows," said Joe, picking up another ornament and pretending to look at the

markings on the bottom of it.

"Over here, Joe!" squawked Petey.

He was fluttering around a bookcase in the corner of the room. On the top was a large vase with flowers painted on it.

"I can see something inside!" cried Petey.

Joe grabbed a chair and pushed it over to the bookcase.

"What are you doing?" gasped Matt.

"Just checking . . . I think that's a very rare vase."

Joe was standing on the chair now, his hands on the vase, when suddenly Pauline appeared in the doorway. "HEY!" she yelled.

Joe jumped in fright and lost his balance. He grabbed the bookcase to steady himself, and it wobbled violently. Joe managed to stop himself from falling, but the vase shook, then fell forward. He tried to catch it, but it slipped through his fingers and crashed to the ground.

UNDEAD PETS

Pauline's mouth opened, but no words came out. Joe looked at the vase in horror. It lay on the floor in pieces.

"What was that noise?" called Maggie from the kitchen.

"The boy broke one of your vases!" Pauline yelled back.

"Joe!" said Mom, appearing behind Pauline, her scissors still in her hand.

"I can explain," said Joe in a small voice.

"He thought the vase was an antique," said Matt, trying to help.

Joe looked at his shoes. "I'm really sorry . . ."

"I'll expect my haircut for free now!" yelled Maggie from the kitchen.

CHAPTER EIGHT

"It was there, I saw it!" shrieked Petey. He was sitting on Joe's shoulder as they walked back to the car. "The raffle ticket was lying in the broken bits of vase!"

Joe nodded. He'd seen it, too. And so had Pauline. She'd put it in her pocket when she thought no one was looking. But there was nothing Joe could do about it now. Mom had sent him and Matt to wait in the car.

"I told you not to touch anything," grumbled Matt.

Joe nodded miserably.

"Do you think your mom will still pay us?" asked Matt.

"I doubt it," he said. But getting paid for delivering Mom's flyers was the least of his worries!

"What are we going to do now?" wailed Petey.

Joe shrugged. Even if he had a plan, which he didn't, it wasn't as if he could discuss it now—not in front of Matt.

Petey tucked his head under his wing and began babbling, *"Pat-a-cake, pat-a-cake, baker's man, bake me a cake as fast as you can!"*

"How could you?" said Mom, getting into the driver's seat and slamming the car door behind her. "Not only did I have to do the cut for free, but I'm sure Maggie Pringle will tell all her neighbors what happened. I'll never get work on this street again!"

"Sorry, Mom."

"Sorry, Mom, sorry, Mom! Silly Joe!" Petey chirped.

Joe wished Petey would put a sock in it!

"You know you shouldn't touch other people's property!" said Mom.

"Maybe you could buy her another vase," suggested Matt. "There's that sale at Beddows tomorrow—they've got tons of horrible vases."

Mom scowled. "Thanks, Matt, but I don't think that will help."

Joe sat up straight. Actually, making sure he was at Beddows at the same time as Pauline Pringle might not be a bad thing. Perhaps there was still a chance he could stop her from claiming the raffle prize. He wasn't sure how, but if he could come up with something . . .

"Please, could I buy Ms. Pringle something else?" pleaded Joe. "I've still got some of my birthday money left. I'd like to get her something to make up for the vase."

Mom sighed. "It's a nice idea, Joe, but—"

Just then there was a knock on Mom's car window. It was Sarah.

"Gabriella's mom says she'd like a haircut!" she said, smiling proudly. "In fact, her whole family wants one!"

Joe made a face.

"Well done, Sarah!" Mom beamed.

"Guess I got more customers than you, Joe. I win!"

Joe didn't say anything. He was hoping Mom wouldn't tell Sarah about the vase. If she did, he'd never hear the end of it.

"What's the plan?" asked Petey. He was perched on the mirror as Joe brushed his teeth.

"I dunno." Joe spat out a mouthful of toothpaste. He'd been trying to come up with a new plan all day, but he hadn't gotten anywhere.

"Dunno! Dunno!" repeated Petey. Then he caught sight of himself in the mirror and pecked his reflection. "Who's a pretty boy? Beautiful Petey!"

Joe put his toothbrush back in the holder. "Maybe I could just wait until Pauline's about to get her prize, and then shout out something about it being the wrong sister."

Petey cocked his feathered head to one

side. "Would that work?"

"Doubt it! I'd probably get into even more trouble with Mom, too."

"Why can't you just tell Maggie she's the winner?"

Joe wiped his mouth on the towel. "Because she'd want to know how I found out!" He sighed. "I can hardly tell her that her undead bird told me! If only someone else could tell her—like the manager of the department store." He froze. "Maybe he could!"

"What?" Petey blinked at him. "How?"

"Well, it wouldn't actually be the manager. It would be me! I could pretend to be calling from the store to tell her she's the winner!"

Petey gave a shriek. "Great plan, Joe!"

"There's one problem. I don't sound like a grown-up. My voice isn't deep enough." Joe frowned. "Unless I could change my voice somehow."

"How?"

"I know! Follow me!" Joe raced out of the bathroom and down the hall to Toby's room. He pushed the door open slowly . . .

A light immediately went out and Toby dived back into bed, burrowing under the covers.

"It's all right, it's me!" Joe said.

Toby peeked out. "Oh, hi, Joe!"

Joe flicked on the light. Lego bricks were scattered across the floor.

"I wanted to finish building the rocket!" whispered Toby. "Don't tell!"

"I won't," said Joe. "If you let me borrow your voice changer."

"My what?"

"That thing you got for Christmas." Joe pulled open one of Toby's drawers and began rummaging through it. "It was blue, and when you talked into it, it made your voice sound different."

UNDEAD PETS

"I remember!" squeaked Toby. He jumped out of bed and pulled open another drawer.

Petey perched on the curtain rail while the boys searched through Toby's stuff.

"Wow!" Toby said, finding a light-up yo-yo at the back of a drawer. "Look, Joe!"

"Great! But where's the voice changer?" Joe pulled open another drawer.

"HELLO, JOE!" said a robotic voice.

He spun around. Toby was grinning at him, with the voice changer in his hand.

UNDEAD PETS

"I found it!" Toby said proudly.

"Let me see." Joe examined the toy. There were four settings: low, high, alien, and robot. "Stand Back, Earthling!" Joe said, using the alien setting.

Toby giggled.

"Exterminate!" Joe zapped Toby with an imaginary ray gun.

"*Aaah!*" Toby shrieked and dropped to the floor, jerking for a few seconds, then lying still.

"What's going on in here?" Dad stood in the doorway. He looked at Toby, then at the mess of Legos. "Have you been out of bed with your flashlight again, Toby?"

"Sorry. It's my fault," said Joe. "I just came in to borrow something and woke him up."

Dad frowned. "*Mmm,* right!" He smiled. "Okay. Back to bed, both of you!"

Joe raced to his room before Dad could ask any more questions.

CHAPTER NINE

"Tell me the plan again," Petey twittered.

It was Sunday morning and Joe was in the hall, tying his sneakers. Petey was perched on his shoulder.

"We're going to sneak over to Maggie's house," Joe replied.

"Uh-huh!" said Petey.

"Then we'll hide and keep watch until Pauline goes out shopping . . ."

"Uh-huh!" Petey gave another enormous nod—and nearly fell off Joe's shoulder.

"Then I'll call Maggie—you gave me the number, remember . . ."

"Petey Pringle, 29 Argyll Avenue, telephone number 555-6283."

"Yeah, that's it!" said Joe.

"Petey Pringle, 29 Argyll Avenue, telephone number 555-6283."

"Yeah, I got it, Petey!"

"Petey Pringle, 29 Argyll A—"

"Stop!" said Joe, and he clapped his hands.

Petey gave himself a shake. "Sorry."

"Then I'll use the voice changer to pretend to be the manager calling from the store. I'll tell Maggie that she's won the raffle prize and that she has to come and collect it!"

"Great plan, Joe!"

"Yeah." Joe stood up. "It is. But first I have to get my hands on a cell phone."

Joe wasn't allowed to have his own cell phone until he went to middle school, the same as Sarah.

Undead Pets

"Of course!" Joe said suddenly. "I'll borrow Sarah's!" He could hear the shower going. "Her phone will be in her room," he said. "Come on!"

He sneaked past the bathroom, down the hall, and into Sarah's room.

Joe held his nose. Sarah liked really stinky perfume. The room was cluttered with makeup and hair products, and the walls were covered in posters for vampire movies. Joe felt his heart pounding. He was never—NOT EVER!—

allowed in Sarah's room. If he got caught, she'd go ballistic.

He spotted Sarah's phone on her bedside table. As he reached for it, it beeped. Joe jumped. But it was just a text message.

Petey was twittering nervously above Joe's head, swinging back and forth on Sarah's purple lampshade.

Joe pocketed the phone and crept out of the room as quickly as he could. Then he grabbed the voice changer from his room and bounded down the stairs.

"Back in a bit, Mom!" he yelled. "Just got to take something to Matt!"

He slammed the door behind him, jumped on his bike, and set off with Petey still clinging to his shoulder, digging in his claws.

As he skidded to a halt two doors away from Maggie's house, Joe glanced at his watch. "Ten o'clock," he said. "We've got two hours before the presentation in the store. Hopefully Pauline will head out early."

"Pauline loves shopping," cheeped Petey. "Silly Pauline shops till she drops!"

As he spoke, the Pringles' front door opened and Pauline appeared.

"Duck!" Joe yelled. Then he remembered that no one apart from him could actually see Petey. It was only Joe that needed to hide! He dropped down behind a parked car. "Did she see me?" he whispered.

Petey fluttered up to take a look. "Nope! She went the other way."

"Good! We can call Maggie." Joe took out Sarah's cell phone and the voice changer. "Petey, tell me your phone number again."

"Petey Pringle, 29 Argyll Avenue, telephone number 555-6283."

Joe tapped in the numbers. There was a pause, then it started to ring. Joe turned on the speakerphone setting.

"Hello?" Maggie said. "Who is it?"

Joe took a deep breath, then put the voice changer to his lips. "HELLO?" he said. Except he'd pressed the wrong button, and instead of *low,* he'd set it to *alien!*

"Who is this?" Maggie snapped. "What's going on?"

Joe quickly changed the setting on the voice changer, but his hands were shaking now.

"Sorry about that," he said through the voice changer. The low setting sounded better than the alien one, but it was still a bit strange.

"Who is it?" demanded Maggie again.

Joe cleared his throat. "Hello, I'm calling from Beddows department store."

"What?"

"BEDDOWS DEPARTMENT STORE!" Joe boomed.

"Oh yes?" said Maggie, sounding friendlier.

"You've won our raffle!"

"What?"

"Congratulations!"

"I've won?" Maggie sounded shocked.

Joe swallowed again. "Yes . . . and you need to collect your prize from our store today at twelve noon."

There was a pause.

Joe crossed his fingers. What if she didn't believe him? What if she still thought it was a prank?

"Your voice sounds a little bit odd," said Maggie suspiciously.

"The phone isn't working very well!" Joe replied.

"Oh," said Maggie. There was another pause. "And I really won the prize?"

"We sent you a letter," said Joe.

"What letter? I didn't get a letter."

Joe thought he'd better hang up now. "Not to worry, see you at noon. Good-bye." He quickly ended the call. Petey was fluttering around him nervously. "Do you think she believed me?"

"I'll go and see!"

"But how can you get in?" called Joe. Then he remembered—Petey was an undead pet. He didn't need an invitation! Joe watched him fly straight through the wall of the house.

The phone beeped. It was another text message. He wondered how crazy his sister was going right now, looking for her lost phone.

In a blink Petey was back. "Maggie is putting on her coat!"

"Really?" Joe grinned at the parakeet. "She believed me, then?"

Petey nodded. "And she went looking for her raffle ticket. I don't think she could remember where she'd put it, then she spotted the gap where the vase that you broke used to be and suddenly she looked a bit annoyed. I heard her say 'Pauline' in an angry voice."

"Do you think she suspects Pauline of stealing it?"

Petey shrugged.

Just then, they heard the Pringles' door opening again. Joe ducked behind the car. "What's happening?" he hissed.

Petey fluttered up to look. "Maggie is locking the front door. She's going the same way Pauline went!"

"We did it!" Joe whispered. He punched the air victoriously.

"JOE EDMUNDS! What are you doing

here?" said a horribly familiar voice.

Joe gasped. It was Gabriella. She stood glowering at Joe, tossing her blond curls and twisting her mouth into a nasty sneer.

"I . . ." Joe felt his face turn bright red. "I was just delivering the rest of the flyers for my mom, but I fell off my bike."

Gabriella's eyes narrowed. "I thought Sarah already delivered the rest of the flyers."

Joe climbed back onto his bike without answering. "Got to go!" he said.

"Tell Sarah I've been texting her," yelled Gabriella.

Joe pedaled away as fast as he could.

CHAPTER TEN

"Where have you been, Joe?" Mom was waiting for him in the hall, tapping her watch. "We're supposed to be going shopping this morning, remember?"

"Well, I'm not going anywhere until I find my phone," bellowed Sarah from the living room.

Joe felt his cheeks burning. The phone was in his pocket. "Does she have to come?" he whispered to Mom.

"Sarah needs new school shoes. I might as well get them at the sale."

UNDEAD PETS

"Where is it?" he heard Sarah shriek. She was thundering around the house like an angry elephant, turning everything upside down.

"Mom!" yelled Toby. "Sarah just shoved me off the sofa!"

"I'm checking down the side of the cushions!" she shouted. "Joe? Where's Joe? I bet he stole it!"

Joe tiptoed upstairs.

"You can't just accuse your brother," he heard Mom say. "You need to take more care of your possessions, Sarah!"

Joe ran the rest of the way, straight into the bathroom. He shut the door, then took out the phone and put it down next to Sarah's toothbrush.

"What are you doing?" asked Petey, who'd appeared through the wall.

"Just watch," he said. "SARAH!" he yelled.

"WHAT?"

"I just found your phone in the bathroom!"

There was a pause. "But I didn't leave it there!"

They got to the department store just before twelve.

"I'm going to look at the clothes," said Sarah sulkily.

"No, let's go to the shoe department first," said Mom.

"Joe!" squawked Petey suddenly. "There's Pauline!"

She was on the escalator, heading upstairs.

"Quick!" said Petey. "We need to follow her."

Joe glanced around. Maggie should be there by now, too. He looked at his watch—only a couple of minutes to go until the prize would be awarded.

UNDEAD PETS

"Dad?" said Joe.

"*Mmm?*"

"Want some free cake?"

Joe pointed to a large sign nearby:

RAFFLE DRAWING!
Free cake in Beddows Café
Second floor at 12 noon.

Toby's eyes lit up.

Joe headed for the escalator, and Petey flew off ahead. Toby ran to follow.

"Slow down, Joe!" called Dad. "No! Toby! Stay with me!"

His little brother stopped and waited for Dad, but Joe pretended he hadn't heard him. He scrambled up the moving steps,

dodging past the other shoppers.

"Careful!" called an old man.

"Sorry, sorry!" called Joe as he passed the other people.

"Over there!" squawked Petey.

Joe jumped off the top step of the escalator and dashed over to the café, where a man in a sharp suit was standing next to a photographer. A crowd of customers was waiting in front of them. Joe could see Pauline in the middle. But there was no sign of Maggie.

"Thank you so much for coming to Beddows today," the man in the suit said, "and for helping us to celebrate fifty years of business. As a special thank-you to all our loyal customers, we'll be serving cake in a moment. But first we'd like to present our grand raffle prize—a five-hundred-dollar gift certificate to use in the store."

There was a round of applause. Joe could

see Pauline straightening her coat, getting ready to go up and claim the prize.

"Where's Maggie?" shrieked Petey. He was fluttering around the group. "I can't see Maggie!"

"And the winner of the grand prize drawing is . . . Ms. Maggie Pringle!"

"That's me!" said Pauline, waving Maggie's raffle ticket in the air. "I'm Maggie Pringle!"

"No, you're not!" shrieked Petey helplessly. He fluttered toward Pauline as though he was about to peck her nose!

But just then another voice repeated what Petey had said.

"NO, YOU'RE NOT!" Joe spun around to see who was speaking. "I'm Maggie Pringle!"

The real Maggie Pringle was standing at the top of the escalator. Her hair was messed up, and her cheeks were red. She looked like she'd been running.

A look of pure horror passed over Pauline's face. Her mouth dropped open. "I . . . I . . . ," she muttered.

The customers looked from Pauline to Maggie, then back again.

The store manager looked at the photographer, then at Maggie and Pauline. "Who is Maggie Pringle?" he asked the two sisters.

"*She* is!" Joe heard himself shout, pointing

to Maggie. "The lady with the frizzy hair!"

He clamped his hand over his mouth. He hadn't meant to sound rude.

But Maggie smiled at him and marched forward. "I'm Maggie Pringle. I got held up—my bus broke down. That woman is my sister!"

"Is that true?" asked the manager. He didn't look like he wanted to argue with Maggie.

"Yes," said Pauline in a small voice. "I thought I should pick up Maggie's prize for her, because I . . . didn't think she was going to be here today!"

Maggie's face was thunderous. "Really!" she said. "Well, that's probably because I didn't get the letter they sent me!"

Pauline gulped. Her face turned crimson.

"Thank goodness you called me," said Maggie, smiling at the store manager.

He looked puzzled. "But, I didn't—"

"Can we have a picture of Maggie with her prize, please?" said the photographer.

Joe breathed a sigh of relief.

A waitress appeared pushing a large cart packed with cake.

"I don't mind if I do," said Dad, who'd appeared with Toby. He took a slice of cake from the waitress, then turned to Joe. "You shouldn't have run off like that," Dad said. "I had to find Mom and Sarah to tell them where we were going!"

"Sorry, Dad." Joe took a slice of cake.

"We did it!" cheeped Petey, landing on Joe's shoulder, his chest puffed up with pride. "We saved Maggie's money!"

"Do you think she'll forgive Pauline for stealing her letter?" Joe whispered.

Petey shrugged. "Sisters! Can't live with 'em, can't live without 'em!"

Joe giggled.

Just then, Sarah appeared. She marched up to the dessert cart and helped herself to the largest slice of cake she could find.

"Bye, Joe," chirped Petey. "Thanks for everything."

Joe looked around, but Petey had already vanished. A small green feather fluttered down. Joe caught it and held it in his palm.

"Hello, Joe!" It was Maggie Pringle. "Thanks for speaking up for me just now."

"That's okay." Joe looked at his feet, hoping that Ms. Pringle wasn't going to get mad at him for saying she had frizzy hair.

But she didn't. "Doing some shopping?" she asked.

"I was going to get you another vase," said Joe.

"Don't worry about that. I can buy plenty of vases now—I just won the raffle!"

Pauline sidled past, looking miserable.

"I might even treat my sister to something!" said Maggie in a loud voice.

Pauline's face lit up. "Really?"

"I saw some nice porcelain parakeet figurines," Maggie added. "I thought we could buy a matching pair to remind us of Petey!"

Gifts and China ⇨